Discover and Explore

BASED ON **TIMOTHY GOES TO SCHOOL** AND OTHER STORIES BY

ROSEMARY WELLS

ILLUSTRATED BY MICHAEL KOELSCH

VIKING

Jacket and interior illustrations copyright © Rosemary Wells, 2001 • Interior illustrations by Michael Koelsch • Text copyright © Penguin Putnam Inc., 2001
Educational consultant: John F. Savage, Ed.D. • All rights reserved • Library of Congress Catalog Card Number: 00-068341 • ISBN: 0-670-91035-X

Hilltop School

DORIS

NORA

CLAUDE

FRANK

FRANK

"**TODAY** we are going to plant seeds," says Mrs. Jenkins. She passes out paper cups filled with soil and gives everyone a tiny seed. "What does a seed need to grow into a plant?" Mrs. Jenkins asks.

"I know. Soil," says Yoko. "And sun."

"That's right," says Mrs. Jenkins. "Plants use soil and sunshine to get their food. What else do they need?"

"Water!" Claude calls out. "I help my mom water the plants at home.

"Yes," says Mrs. Jenkins. "I'll pour a little water into each of your cups after you plant your seeds."

Look at the picture on the next page. What will Charles, Yoko, and Doris need to plant their seeds?

 The Next Step

Follow Mrs. Jenkins's instructions and plant your own seed. Don't forget to put it in a sunny place and give it water once a week.

"Plants are alive," says Mrs. Jenkins. "Like all living things, plants grow, move, and make other living things. What else is alive?"

"Birds are alive," says Fritz.

"Bugs are alive," says Doris.

"We are alive!" says Nora.

"Right," says Mrs. Jenkins. "What isn't alive?"

"Plastic flowers aren't alive," says Timothy. "They might look real, but they don't grow."

"A car isn't alive," says Yoko. "It can't move on its own—it needs someone to drive it."

Look at the pictures on the next page. Tell whether each thing is living or not.

The Next Step

Take a walk through your neighborhood. What do you see that is living? What do you see that is not living? How can you tell the difference?

"This is called an incubator," says Mrs. Jenkins. "Inside the incubator there are four eggs, and inside the eggs there are baby chicks. The incubator keeps the eggs warm until the chicks are ready to come out."

"Is that how chickens are born?" Charles asks.

"Not always," says Mrs. Jenkins. "Usually a mother hen sits on her eggs to keep them warm until the chicks are ready to hatch. But since we don't have a mother hen here, the incubator will work just as well."

"This is going to be fun!" says Yoko.

Over the next few weeks, everyone looks into the incubator every day to see if any chicks have hatched. Look at the picture of the incubator on the next page. How many of the chicks have already hatched? Which egg do you think will hatch next? Which egg do you think will be the last to hatch?

 The Next Step

Once the chicks hatch, they will be taken out of the incubator and brought to a farm. Can you name some other animals that live on a farm?

"All living things grow," says Mrs. Jenkins. "You are all living, so you are all growing. You have grown a lot already."

"I saw a picture of myself when I was a baby," says Yoko. "I was so little!"

"I was little, too," says Timothy.

"I'm still little!" says Charles.

"You all have a lot of growing to do," says Mrs. Jenkins, "and you'll all get bigger and taller."

Find the pictures on the next page of Yoko, Timothy, and Charles when they were babies, and the pictures of them now. How have they changed? In which pictures are they bigger? In which pictures are they smaller?

 The Next Step

Keep track of how much you are growing. Ask an adult to measure how tall you are and write down your height and the date you were measured. Measure your height every month and see how much you grow.

"There are five senses that help us learn about the world," says Mrs. Jenkins. "Sight, hearing, smell, taste, and touch. Who can tell me some of the ways we use our senses?"

"I can," says Fritz. "We use our eyes to see where we're going."

"We use our hearing when we listen to each other talk," says Claude.

"We use our noses to smell food," say the Franks, "and we use our mouths to taste it."

"Good," says Mrs. Jenkins. "What else?"

"We use our hands to touch things," says Nora.

Look at the pictures of Timothy and his friends on the next page. Point to the child using the sense of . . .

SIGHT   **HEARING**   **SMELL**   **TASTE**   **TOUCH**

 ### The Next Step

Which sense do you use when you are listening to music? Which senses do you use when you eat breakfast? Which senses do you use when you watch a movie?

13

SUNDAY	MONDAY	TUESDAY	WEDNESDAY	THURSDAY	FRIDAY	SATURDAY

Mrs. Jenkins's class kept a weather chart for a week. The chart shows how many sunny days, how many cloudy days, and how many rainy days there were in the week. Look at the chart. How many sunny days were there? How many cloudy days were there? How many rainy days were there? Were there more rainy days or sunny days?

The Next Step

When people ask, "What's it like outside?" they're asking about the weather. Look at the weather chart Mrs. Jenkins's class made. What was it like on Monday? What was it like on Friday? Look out the window. What is it like outside right now?

"The weather affects us in different ways," Mrs. Jenkins tells the class. "Who can tell me how the weather changes what we do?"

"When it's hot, we can go swimming," says Timothy. "And when it snows, we can make snowmen."

"When it's raining, we carry umbrellas," says Claude.

"And jump in puddles!" say the Franks.

Look at the pictures below. What kind of weather are Doris, Timothy, and Yoko dressed for?

 **The Next Step**

When the weather changes, so does the temperature outside. When it is hot, the temperature is high. When it is cold, the temperature is low. What is the temperature right now? Is it hot outside or cold?

"There are four seasons in each year: spring, summer, fall, and winter," Mrs. Jenkins tells the class. "Who knows something about each one?"

"In the spring," says Timothy, "flowers and leaves start to grow."

"Then comes summer," says Claude. "The weather gets hot and we can go to the beach."

"Next is fall," says Nora. "The leaves on some of the trees change color."

"Then it's winter," say the Franks. "The weather gets colder. In some places, it snows."

"Wonderful!" says Mrs. Jenkins. "Take out your crayons and draw a picture showing your favorite season of the year."

Look at the pictures Timothy and his friends drew. Point to each one and say which season is pictured.

 **The Next Step**

What special things do you like to do during each season? Which season is your favorite? Why?

17

"Today we are going to do an experiment," says Mrs. Jenkins. She brings out a tub of water and a box filled with different objects. "We are going to test these things to see whether they sink or float. Everybody please take something out of this box to put into the tub of water."

Claude picks the Ping-Pong ball. "Look!" he says. "It floats."

Charles tries the golf ball. "Oh, no," he says. "It sunk. Why did that happen?"

"The Ping-Pong ball floats because it's full of air and it doesn't weigh much," says Mrs. Jenkins. "The golf ball sank because it's heavy and it doesn't hold any air."

"I'm next!" says Nora. She puts a rock into the tub of water. Do you think it will float or sink? Why? Do you think the other objects in the box will sink or float. Why?

 **The Next Step**

You can do this experiment, too. Ask an adult to help you fill the sink with water. Gather some things to test. Which things sink? Which things float?

18

"It is important to take good care of ourselves," says Mrs. Jenkins. "One way we can do that is by eating right. The food pyramid can help."

"The food pyramid tells us how much of each kind of food we should eat," says Timothy. "We should eat more of the things on the bottom of the pyramid and fewer of the things at the top of the pyramid, right?"

"Right," says Mrs. Jenkins. "Think about something you have eaten today. Where does it go on the food pyramid?"

"We had chicken nuggets for lunch," say the Franks. "They are in the meat group."

"I had carrot sticks for a snack," says Claude. "Carrots are in the vegetables group."

"I had orange juice at breakfast," says Doris. "Orange juice is in the fruit group."

Look at the food pyramid and at the pictures of food at the top of this page. In which group does each food belong on the pyramid?

The Next Step

Do you remember what you ate today? What part of the pyramid does each food you ate today fall into?

FATS, OILS & SWEETS

MILK, YOGURT & CHEESE

MEAT, EGGS & NUTS

VEGETABLES

FRUIT

BREAD, CEREAL, RICE & PASTA

"The earth is our home," says Mrs. Jenkins. "So it's important to take good care of it. What are some ways we can help the earth?"

"We should plant new trees when we cut other trees down," says Timothy. "Because they help keep the air we breathe fresh and clean."

"Turn off water when you're not using it," says Nora. "The earth has a limited amount of water, and we all need to share it."

"Recycle paper, cans, glass, and plastic," say the Franks.

"Don't throw trash on the ground," says Doris. "So the earth stays clean."

"Very good!" says Mrs. Jenkins.

Look at the pictures on the next page. Who is doing something that helps take good care of the earth? Who is not?

The Next Step

If you're in school, ask your teacher if your class can adopt a part of your town and help clean it up. If you're not in school yet, try to be a good recycler. Put paper, cans, glass, and plastic into recycling bins—not into the trash.

Letter to Parents and Educators

The early years are a dynamic and exciting time in a child's life, a time in which children acquire language, explore their environment, and begin to make sense of the world around them. In the preschool and kindergarten years parents and teachers have the joy of nurturing and promoting this continued learning and development. The books in the *Get Set for Kindergarten!* series are designed to help in this wonderful adventure.

The activities in this book were created to be developmentally appropriate and geared toward the interests and abilities of pre-kindergarten and kindergarten children. After each activity, a suggestion is made for "The Next Step," an extension of the skill being practiced. Some children may be ready to take the next step; others may need more time.

Young children are fascinated with the world around them. As they grow and develop, they increase their expanding knowledge of this world by observing, classifying, measuring, experimenting, and otherwise interacting with their environment. *Discover and Explore* provides a springboard for adults and children to talk about the science that is all around us—including plants, animals, seasons, weather, and the earth— to lead children to a greater knowledge and appreciation of the world in which we live.

Throughout the early years, children need to be surrounded by language and learning and love. Those who nurture and educate young children give them a gift of immeasurable value that will sustain them throughout their lives.

John F. Savage, Ed.D.
Educational Consultant